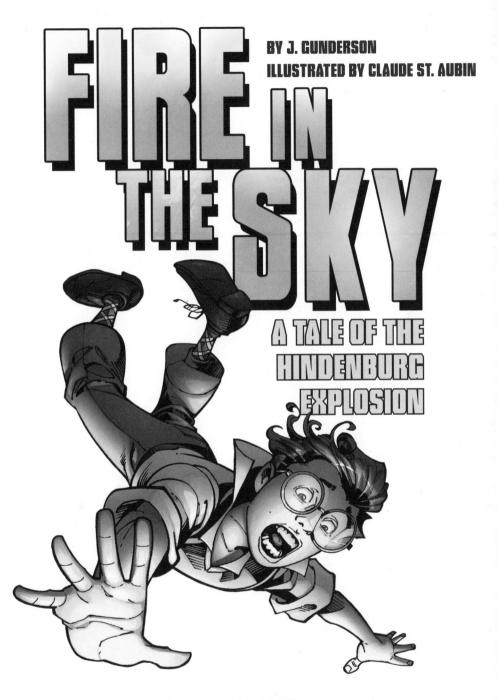

FIRE IN THE SKY

BY J. GUNDERSON

ILLUSTRATED BY CLAUDE ST. AUBIN

A TALE OF THE HINDENBURG EXPLOSION

STONE ARCH BOOKS
www.stonearchbooks.com

Graphic Flash is published by Stone Arch Books
151 Good Counsel Drive, P.O. Box 669
Mankato, Minnesota 56002
www.stonearchbooks.com

Library of Congress Cataloging-in-Publication Data
Gunderson, Jessica.
    Fire in the Sky: A Tale of the Hindenburg Explosion / by Jessica Gunderson;
illustrated by Claude St. Aubin.
    p. cm. — (Graphic Flash)
    ISBN 978-1-4342-1163-7 (library binding)
    ISBN 978-1-4342-1377-8 (pbk.)
    1. Hindenburg (Airship)—Juvenile fiction. [1. Hindenburg (Airship)—Fiction.
2. Germany—History—1933–1945—Fiction.] I. St. Aubin, Claude, ill. II. Title.
PZ7.G963Fi 2009
[Fic]—dc22
                                                          2008032068

Summary: In 1936, 15-year-old Michael Roth and his family are headed toward
America. They're leaving Frankfurt, Germany, to escape the Nazi government
and start a better life. Michael, however, is more excited about the trip than the
destination. They'll be riding aboard the giant *Hindenburg* airship.

Creative Director: Heather Kindseth
Graphic Designer: Brann Garvey

1 2 3 4 5 6 14 13 12 11 10 09

Printed in the United States of America

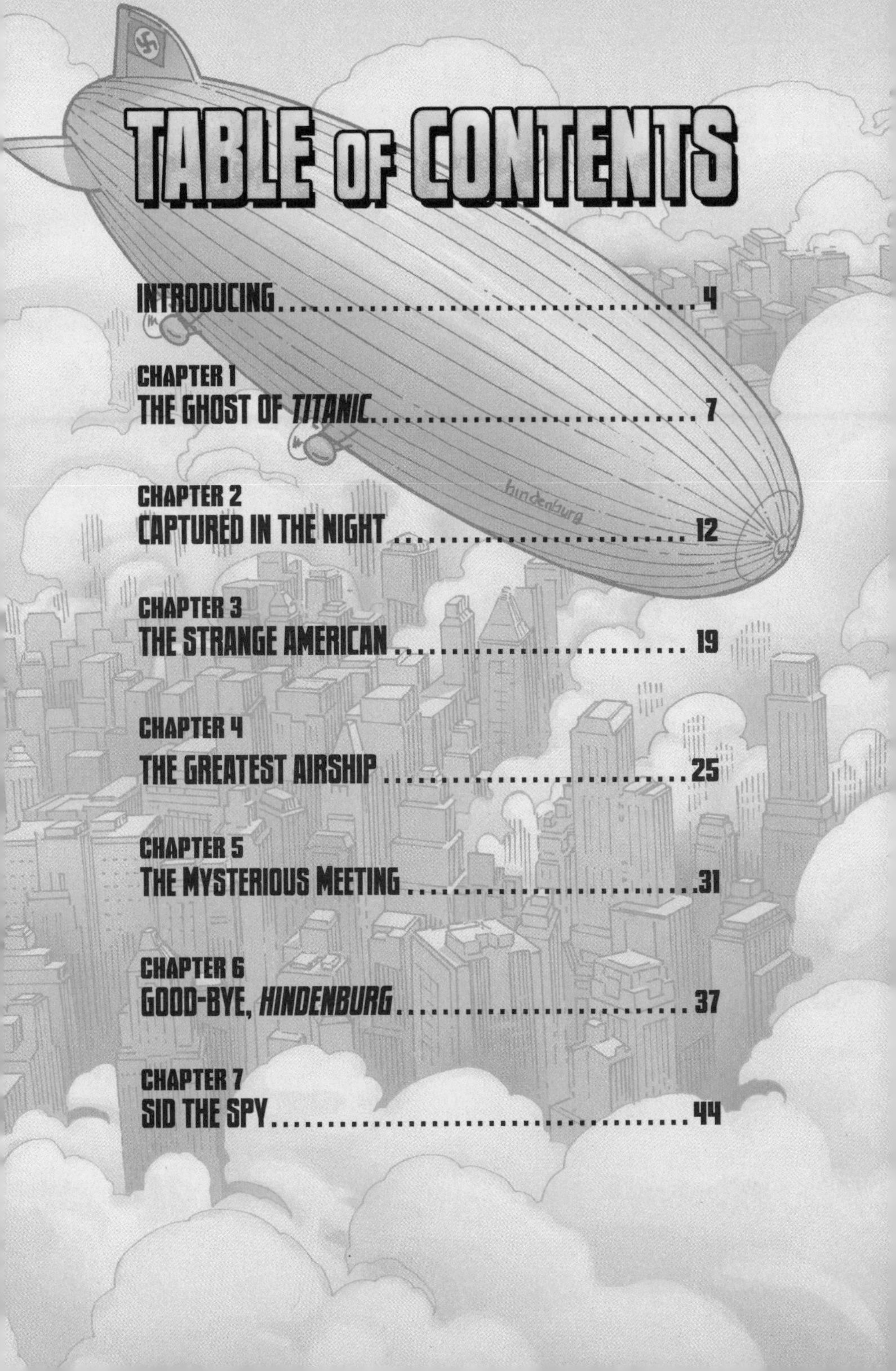

TABLE of CONTENTS

INTRODUCING 4

CHAPTER 1
THE GHOST OF *TITANIC* 7

CHAPTER 2
CAPTURED IN THE NIGHT 12

CHAPTER 3
THE STRANGE AMERICAN 19

CHAPTER 4
THE GREATEST AIRSHIP 25

CHAPTER 5
THE MYSTERIOUS MEETING 31

CHAPTER 6
GOOD-BYE, *HINDENBURG* 37

CHAPTER 7
SID THE SPY 44

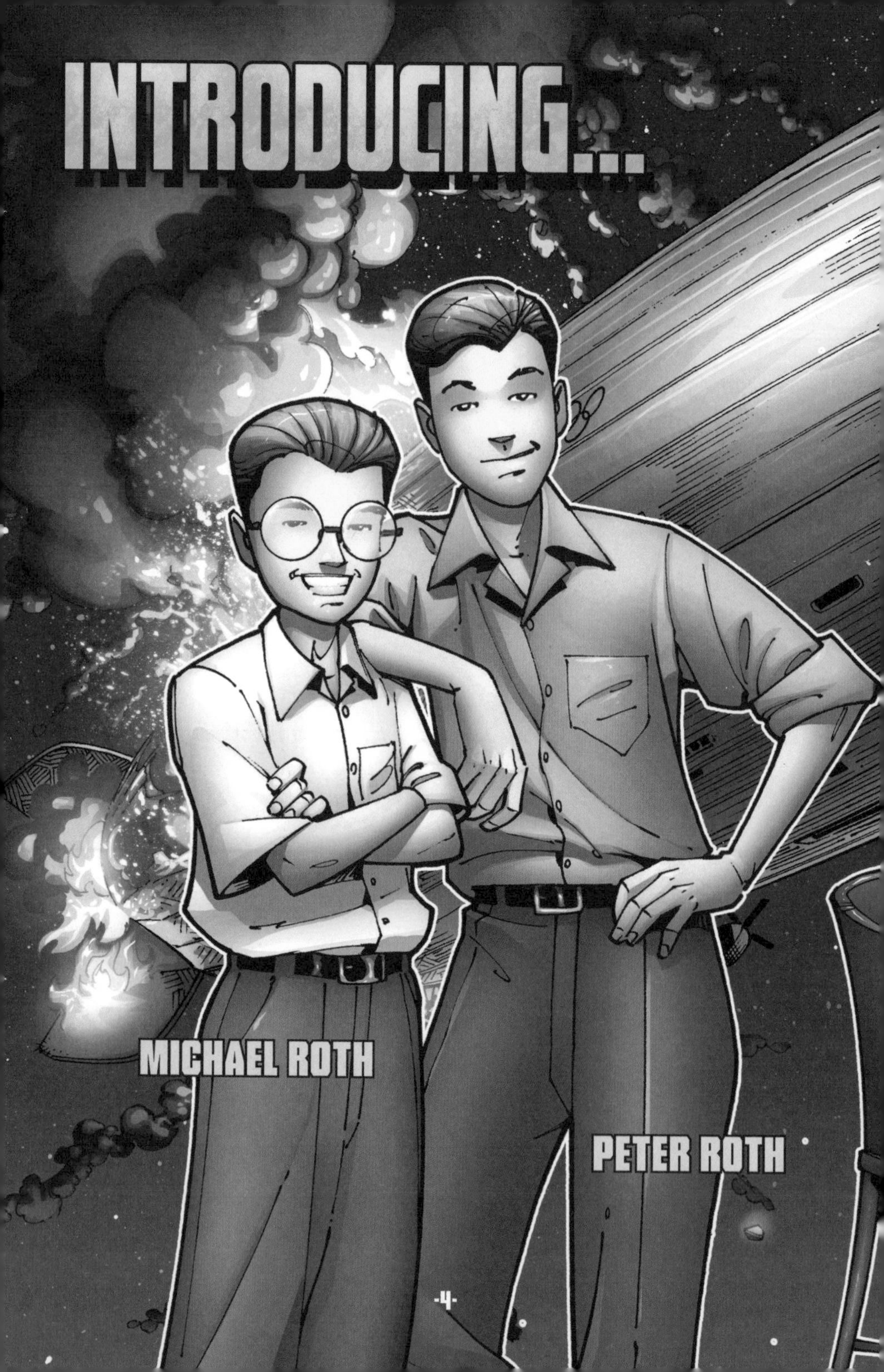
INTRODUCING...
MICHAEL ROTH
PETER ROTH

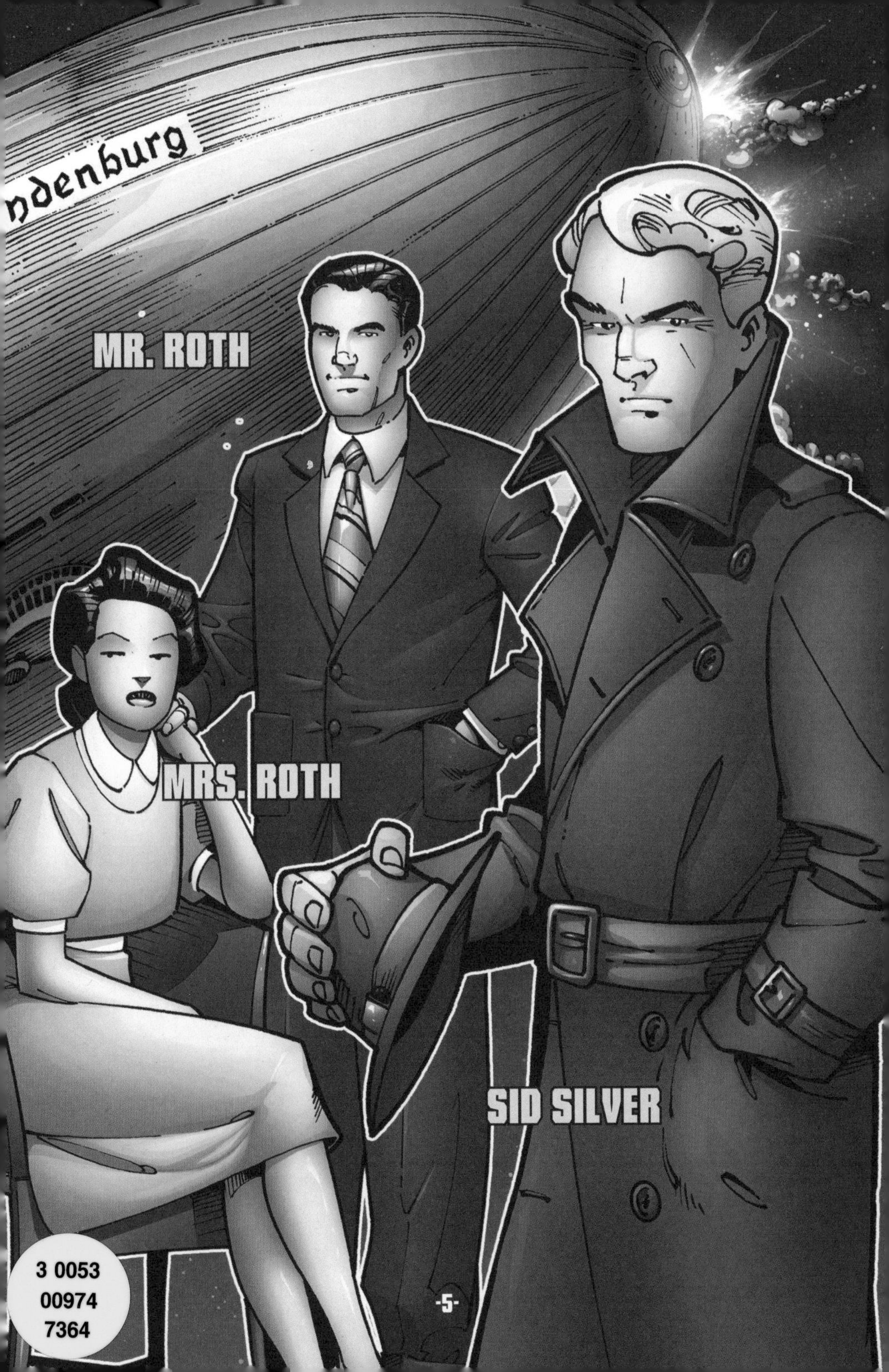
ndenburg
MR. ROTH
MRS. ROTH
SID SILVER

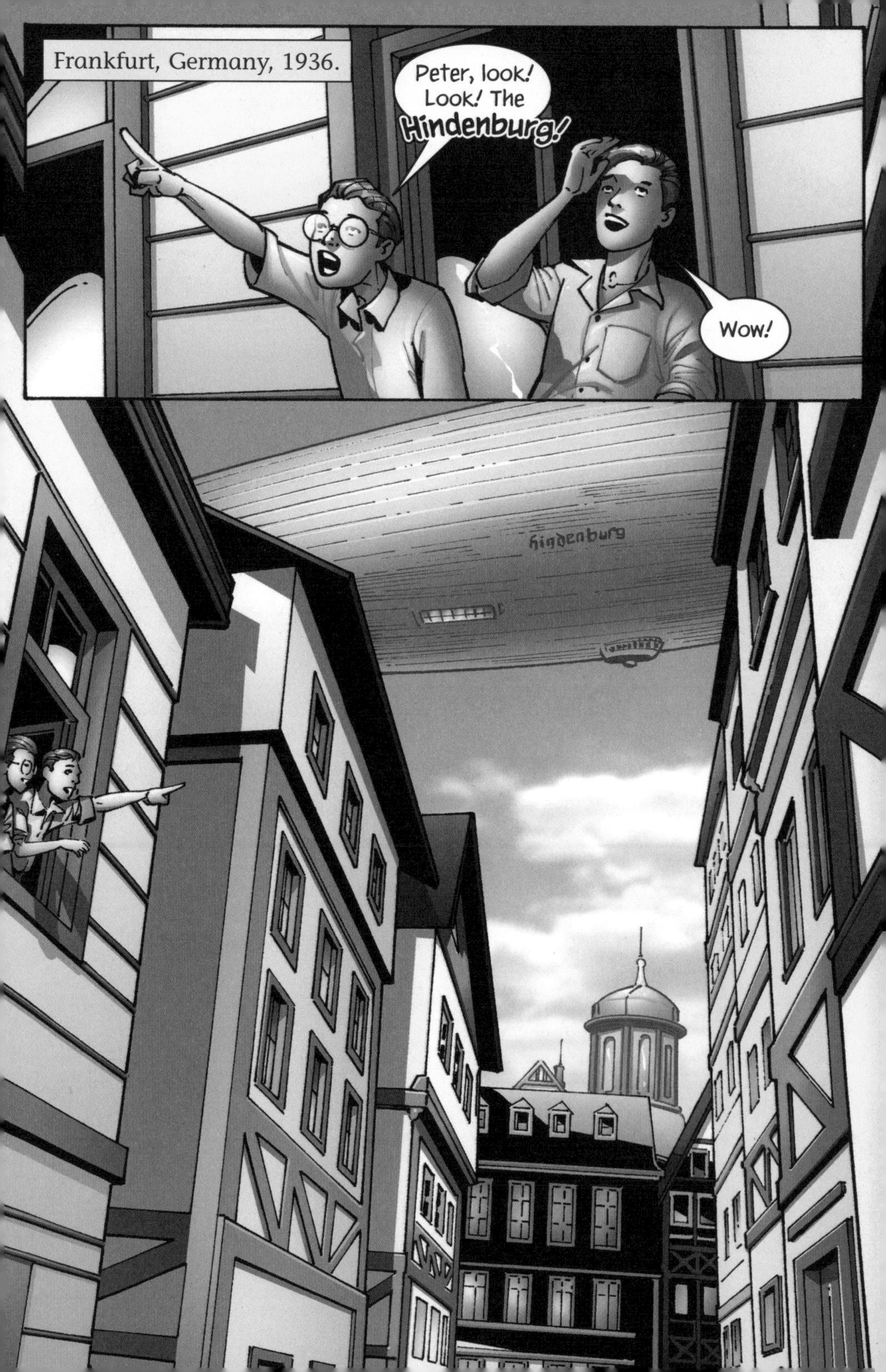
Frankfurt, Germany, 1936.
Peter, look! Look! The Hindenburg!
Wow!
Hindenburg

CHAPTER 1

THE GHOST OF TITANIC

I had the best bedroom in Germany. Well, it would've been the best, if only I didn't have to share it with my brother Peter. He was only a year older, but he acted centuries older.

No, my room was the best because it had a great view. I could see the *Hindenburg*, the greatest airship of all time.

Every time the *Hindenburg* flew, it passed right over our house, right past our bedroom window. The silver airship, or zeppelin, swam like a great whale in the blue sea of the sky.

Through the summer, Peter and I watched as the *Hindenburg* floated overhead, carrying passengers from Germany to America.

When the zeppelin disappeared from view, we returned to our normal, everyday lives. Peter worked on model trains, and I built model ships. We both dreamed of something that would take us far from here, away from our boring life.

Sometimes our friends would come over. But those days were soon gone. By fall, most of our friends had joined Hitler's Youth. Adolph Hitler was the leader of Germany. His youth group was an organization for boys who were interested in the military. Dad didn't like him. He didn't let anyone who was in Hitler's Youth into our house.

Our other friends were Jewish. Mom wouldn't let anyone who was Jewish come over. So it was just Peter and me, left alone upstairs.

Downstairs our parents were always arguing. Dad, who was an American, often spoke so loud you could hear him down the street. Mom, who was German, often tried to calm him.

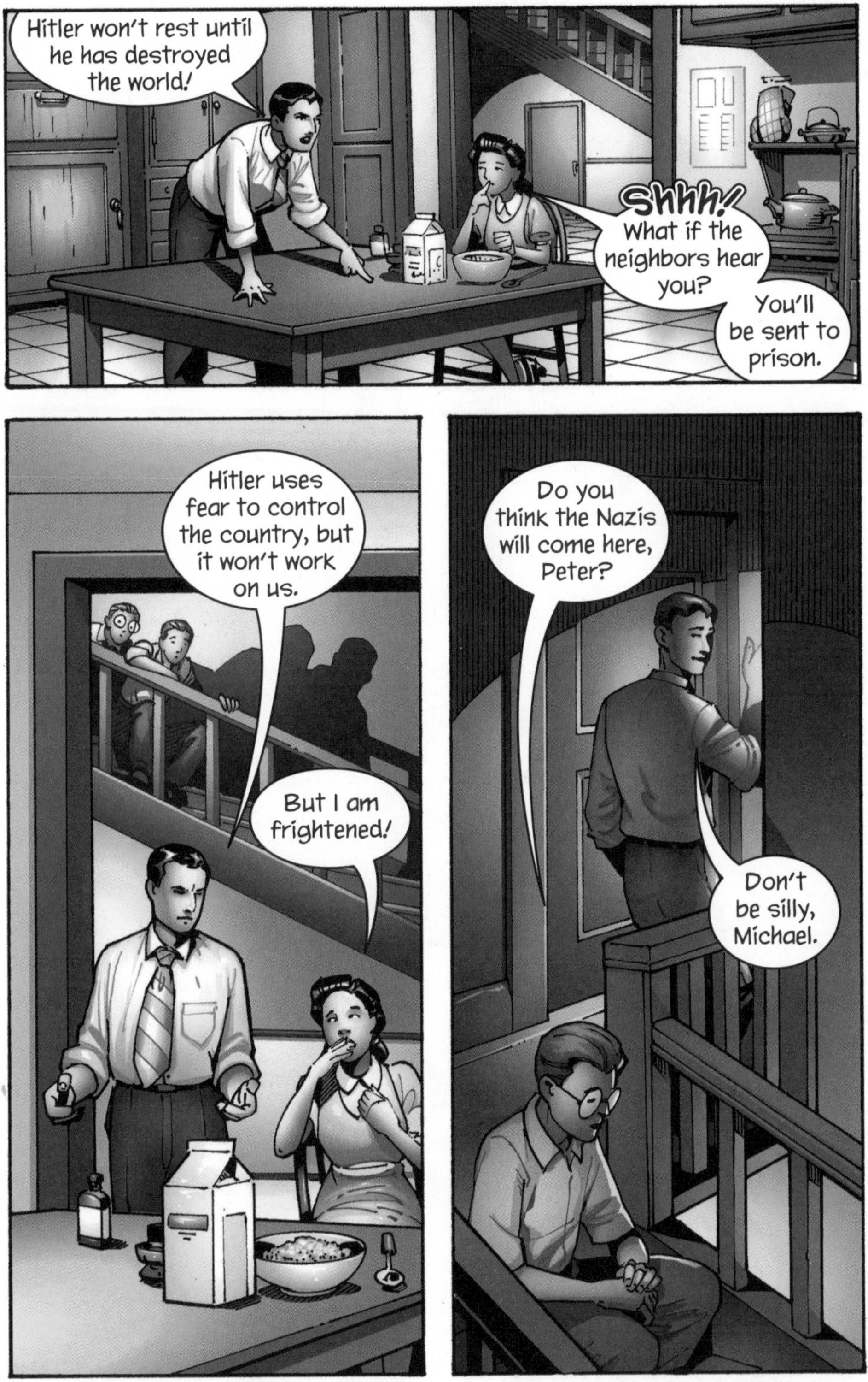
Hitler won't rest until he has destroyed the world!
Shhh! What if the neighbors hear you?
You'll be sent to prison.
Hitler uses fear to control the country, but it won't work on us.
But I am frightened!
Do you think the Nazis will come here, Peter?
Don't be silly, Michael.

Back in my room, I worked on my favorite model ship, the Ghost of the *Titanic*. Dad had been on the real *Titanic* when it sank it 1912. He was just a boy, and he barely survived.

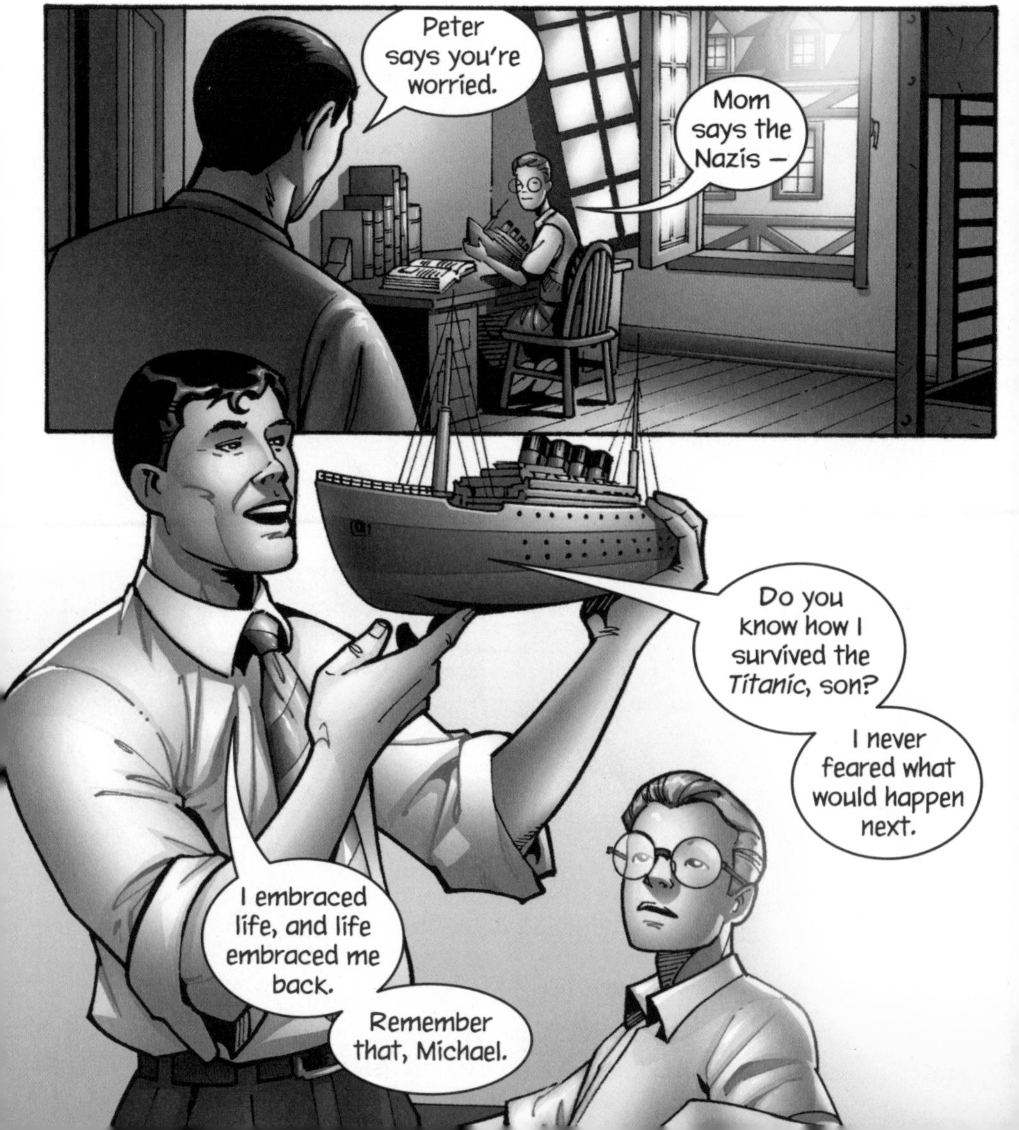
Peter says you're worried.
Mom says the Nazis –
Do you know how I survived the *Titanic*, son?
I never feared what would happen next.
I embraced life, and life embraced me back.
Remember that, Michael.

Whenever Dad told me this story, I shivered. I hoped I'd never be in such danger.

I loved my model ships, but I loved the *Hindenburg* even more. The *Hindenburg* was like a hot air balloon but much larger. It floated because it was filled with hydrogen, a gas that was lighter than air. The *Hindenburg* was like a cruise ship, with a dining room and a lounge. I'd heard there was even a grand piano.

I longed to ride on the great airship.

CHAPTER 2

CAPTURED IN THE NIGHT

The winter of 1936 was the longest of my life. The *Hindenburg* had stopped flying for the season, and I couldn't play with my friend Hans Bernstein anymore because he was Jewish. Hitler's government, the Nazis, made Jewish people ride in different buses from everyone else. They had to go to different schools. Some Jewish people were even sent to prison. Mom said if we were friends with Jews, we could be sent to prison, too.

Every night I listened to their arguments. Dad was mad at Mom for not letting us be friends with Jewish kids. Mom was mad at him for speaking out against Hitler. I wondered if Dad was angry enough to leave Germany. I made up my mind that if Dad ever left, I was going with him.

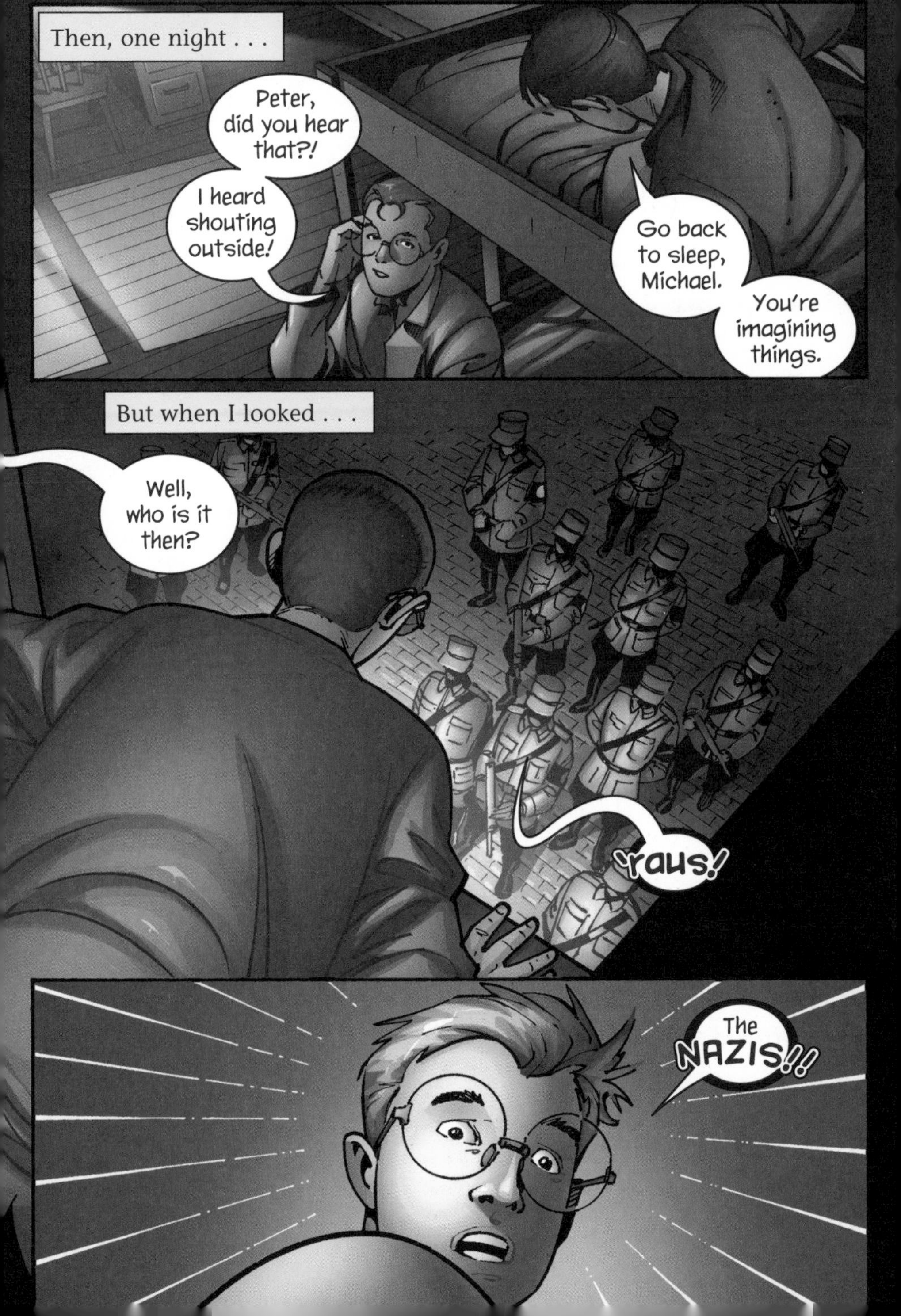
Then, one night . . .
Peter, did you hear that?!
I heard shouting outside!
Go back to sleep, Michael.
You're imagining things.
But when I looked . . .
Well, who is it then?
'raus!
The NAZIS!!

On the sidewalk, a dozen Nazi soldiers stood facing our house. Black, spidery swastikas, the Nazi symbol, colored the shoulders of their uniforms. Guns gleamed against their chests.

Dad stood in front of them.

"What are they doing here?" I whispered. "Dad isn't Jewish."

"No," Peter said. "But he's American."

We strained to hear what Dad was saying to the soldiers. He gestured with his hands, but he didn't look angry. I thought I heard the word *Titanic*, and a flicker of a smile crossed one of the soldier's faces.

Then they grew serious. Dad stopped gesturing. He stopped talking. Two soldiers stepped forward and grabbed his arms.

"No!" I heard my father shout.

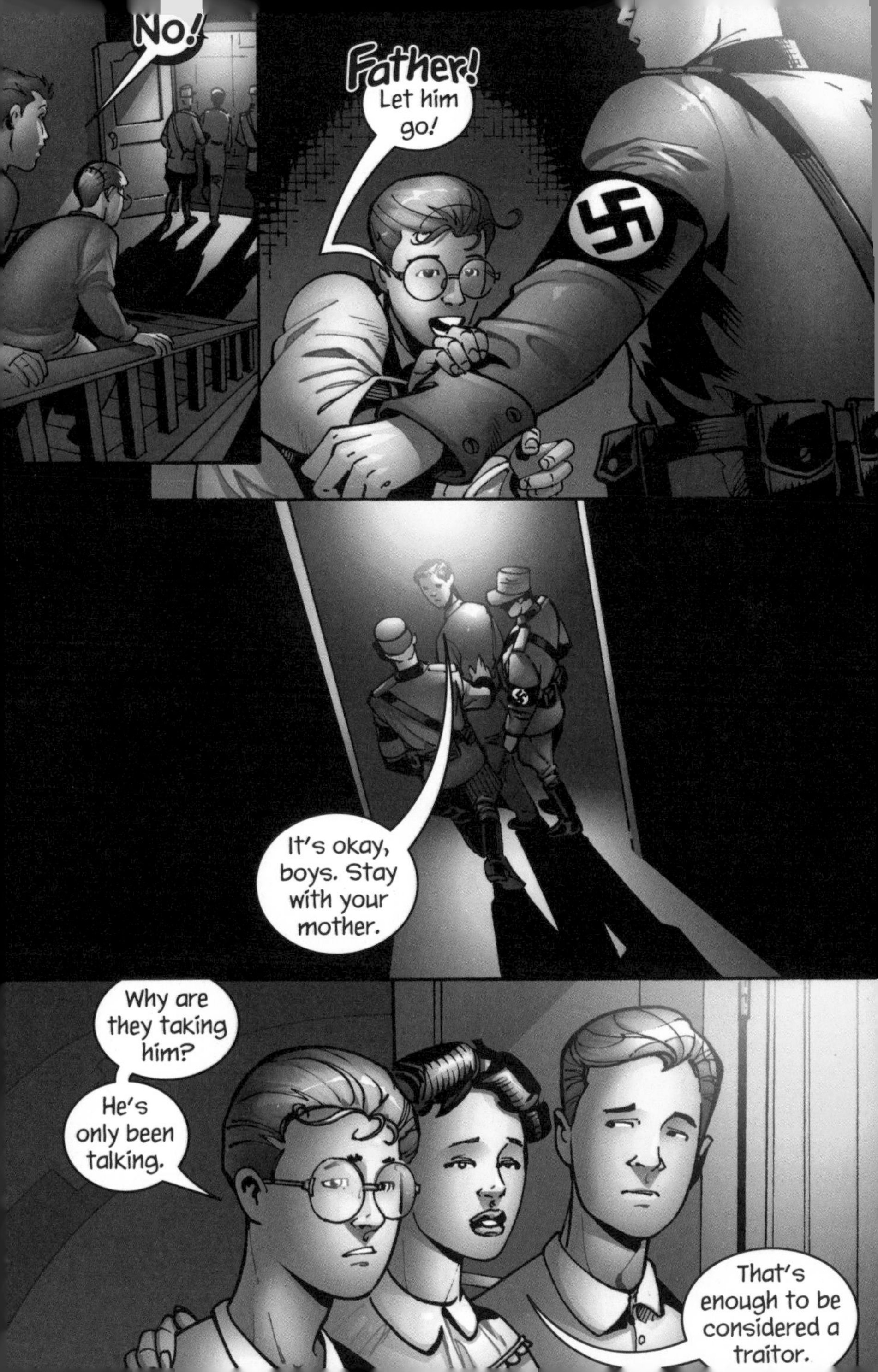
No!
Father!
Let him go!
It's okay, boys. Stay with your mother.
Why are they taking him?
He's only been talking.
That's enough to be considered a traitor.

The next day at school, everyone knew that the Nazis had taken our father. The kids avoided us, and the teacher ignored us when we asked questions about our schoolwork. I suddenly felt what it was like to be Jewish.

I saw Hans Bernstein walking home from school one day. When he saw me, he smiled sadly and kept walking. I tried to catch up. I wanted us to be friends like we used to be.

Then I thought of Dad in one of Hitler's prisons. I knew I couldn't take the risk. The Nazis might be spying on me at this very moment.

Three days after Dad was taken, we were eating breakfast. Suddenly, a long shadow appeared on the floor of the kitchen.

"Dad!" Peter and I rushed to hug him. Mom followed. Her lips were tight, but tears flowed from her eyes.

"What happened, Dad?" I asked. "Did they torture you?"

"Did you get to meet Hitler? Why did they let you go?" Peter said.

Dad laughed, but his laugh was not happy. "How would you like to go to America?" Dad asked.

I couldn't believe my ears. America! I had heard it was a land of mountains, prairies, and huge cities with tall skyscrapers.

"America?" I asked. "For how long?" I glanced at Mom. She stared at her plate.

Dad shrugged. "For a while," he said. "If you like it there, we can stay forever. If you don't like it, you can come back to Germany."

I noticed he didn't say *we* can come back to Germany.

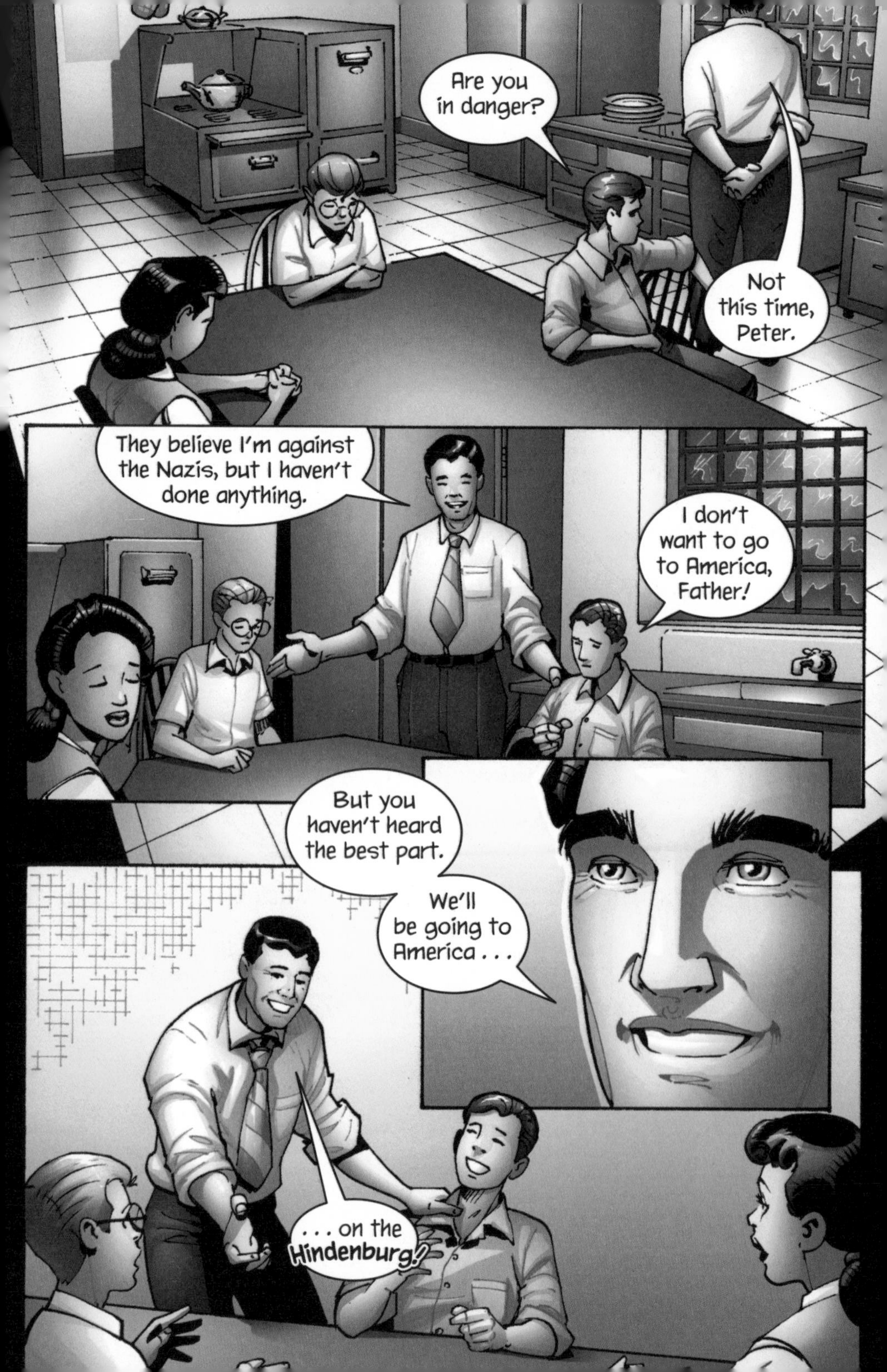
Are you in danger?
Not this time, Peter.
They believe I'm against the Nazis, but I haven't done anything.
I don't want to go to America, Father!
But you haven't heard the best part.
We'll be going to America . . .
. . . on the Hindenburg!

CHAPTER 3

THE STRANGE AMERICAN

I leaned over Peter to stare out the windows of the bus. It was Monday, May 3, 1937, and the bus was taking us from our home in Frankfurt to the airfield, where we would board the *Hindenburg*.

Dad turned in his seat. "Boys, are you ready for an adventure?" he said. "You're about to board the greatest ship ever to sail the skies!"

Even Mom smiled, something she hadn't done much lately. She was going to stay in Germany until we were settled in America. Then she'd cross the Atlantic by sea. She was afraid of flying.

The bus came to an abrupt halt, and we quickly climbed off. I stopped still in my tracks, gasping in awe.

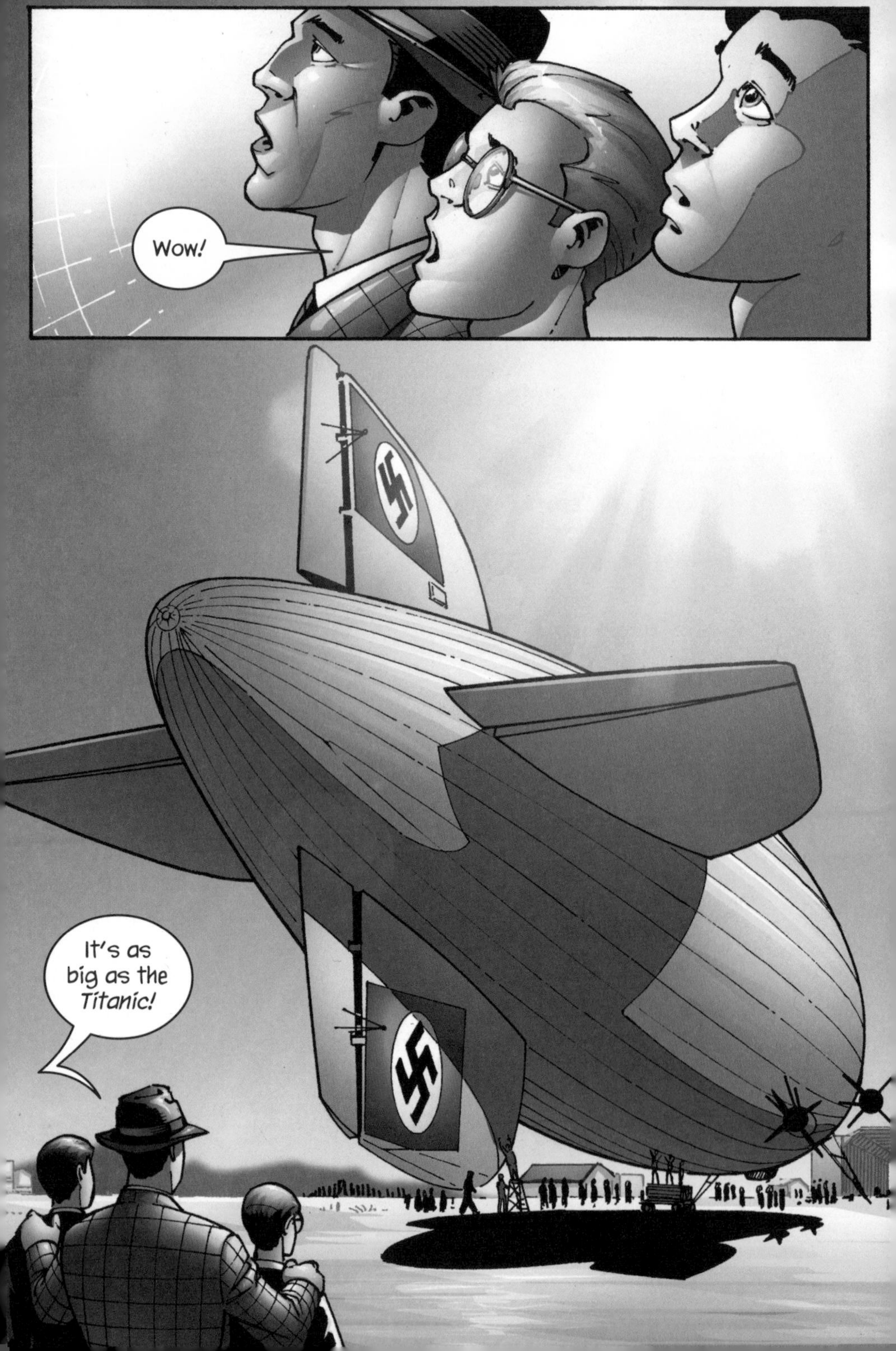
Wow!
It's as big as the *Titanic!*

The *Hindenburg* was built from a metal skeleton. Over the skeleton, silver fabric was stretched tightly. Inside, large balloon-like cells filled with hydrogen allowed it to float. It was hard to believe anything could make the gigantic ship fly.

I stood staring at the *Hindenburg*, unable to take my eyes from it. Then I saw something that sent chills through my bones. Swastikas were painted on the tail fins of the ship.

"Let's go, men!" Dad said cheerily, as though he hadn't noticed the swastikas glaring down at us.

Maybe he hadn't noticed. Swastikas were everywhere in Germany. They were painted on buildings, shown in schools, and sewn onto flags. I used to ignore them, until the night Dad had been taken. Now, the symbol frightened me.

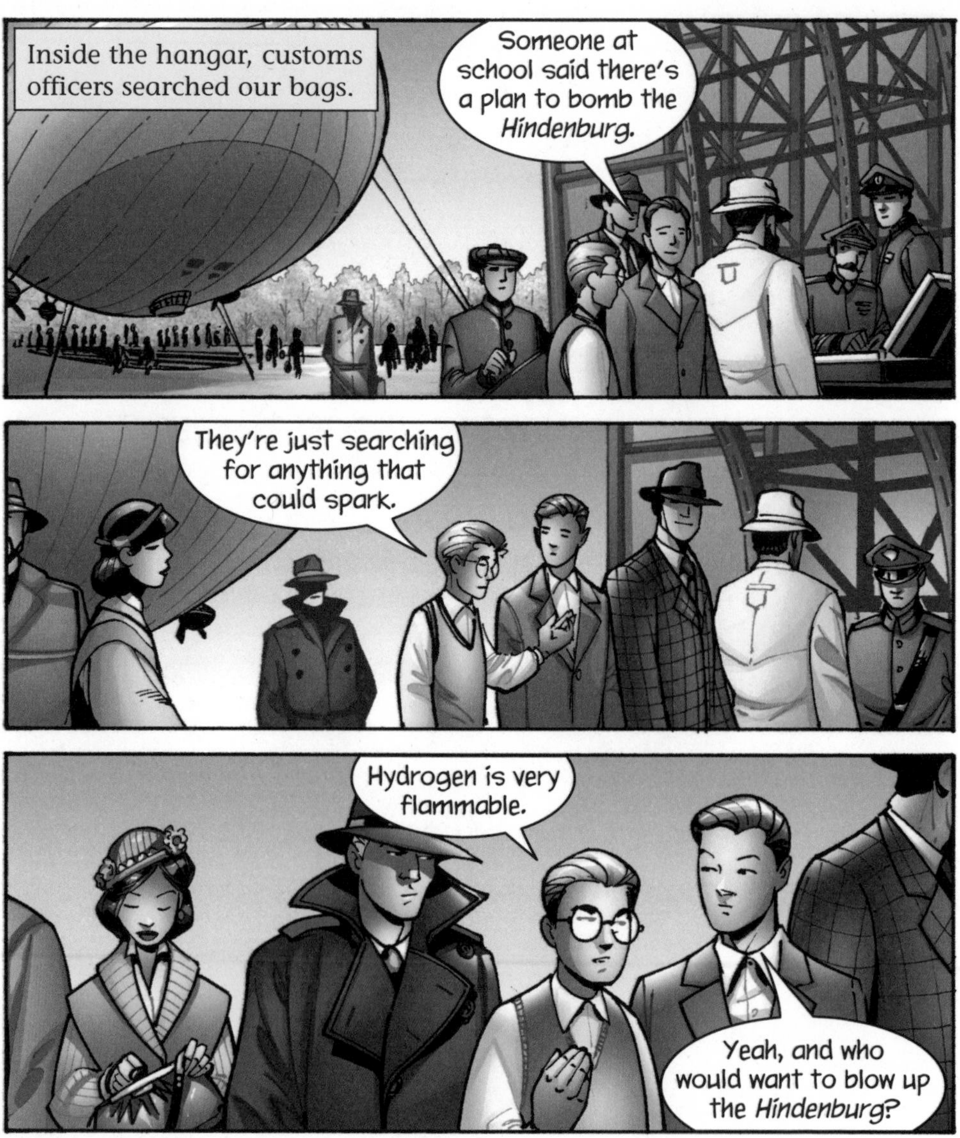
Inside the hangar, customs officers searched our bags.
Someone at school said there's a plan to bomb the *Hindenburg*.
They're just searching for anything that could spark.
Hydrogen is very flammable.
Yeah, and who would want to blow up the *Hindenburg*?

As Peter spoke, I saw a man nearby staring at me. He had a hat and greasy blond hair that hung over his eyebrows. His eyes were dark and narrow as he glared at me. Then he turned away.

"I don't know," Peter answered. "Anyone who doesn't like the Nazis. Americans, I suppose."

We said good-bye to Mom before we boarded the *Hindenburg*. She cried as though she was saying good-bye forever, even though she already had her ticket to America. She hugged Dad for a long time, and then covered his face with kisses. *They do love each other,* I thought.

I felt tiny as we walked under the great airship's shadow. The line of passengers climbing the stairs into the belly of the ship moved slowly. Then I realized why. There was another search.

"I didn't know they are searching us again," a man behind me muttered.

It was the strange blond man I'd seen earlier. He had spoken in English. The man didn't know I could understand English, but my father was American. He must be American, too.

Just then, the customs official grabbed my bag, looking through it quickly. He pulled out my model ship.

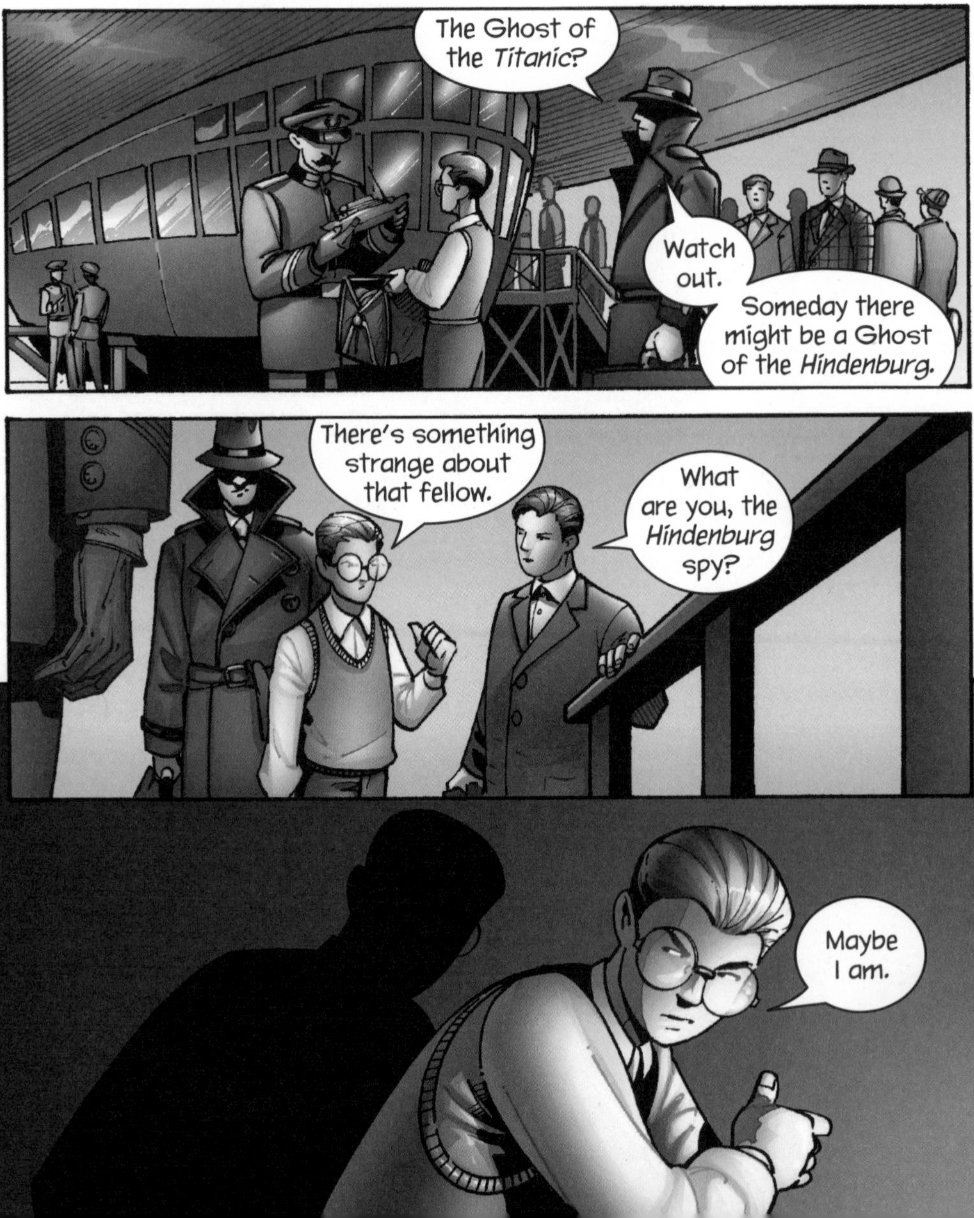
The Ghost of the *Titanic?*
Watch out.
Someday there might be a Ghost of the *Hindenburg.*
There's something strange about that fellow.
What are you, the *Hindenburg* spy?
Maybe I am.

CHAPTER 4

THE GREATEST AIRSHIP

"I heard the Americans want to launch a zeppelin of their own," Peter said as we entered the *Hindenburg*.

"It will never be as big or as fast as the German *Hindenburg*," I said.

I gave a sideways glance at the blond man. He pretended to ignore us.

"Maybe someday I'll be a pilot on an American zeppelin," Peter said. He nodded at Captain Pruss, who was welcoming passengers aboard.

"American? But you're German," I said to Peter.

"Half-German, half-American," Peter corrected. "And we're going to live in America now."

"That's not for certain," I said, but my voice wobbled. The excitement of our *Hindenburg* flight had erased all sadness of leaving Germany. But now the thought struck me. This could be the last time I ever saw German soil.

"Sid Silver!" the captain said to the blond man. "Welcome aboard!"

Sid Silver, I thought. *Sounds like an American spy name to me.*

The inside of the *Hindenburg* was as grand as the outside. It hardly seemed like we were on an airship. Hallways ran down both sides of the ship, past a dining room on the port side and the lounge on the starboard side.

"Top bunk!" Peter cried as we reached our cabin. The cabin had bunk beds and a small sink.

"You always get top bunk," I grumbled.

"No time to argue," he said. "We're about to take off."

We raced down to the row of windows on the port side of the ship. There we saw our father among the other passengers, waiting for liftoff.

I stopped in surprise.

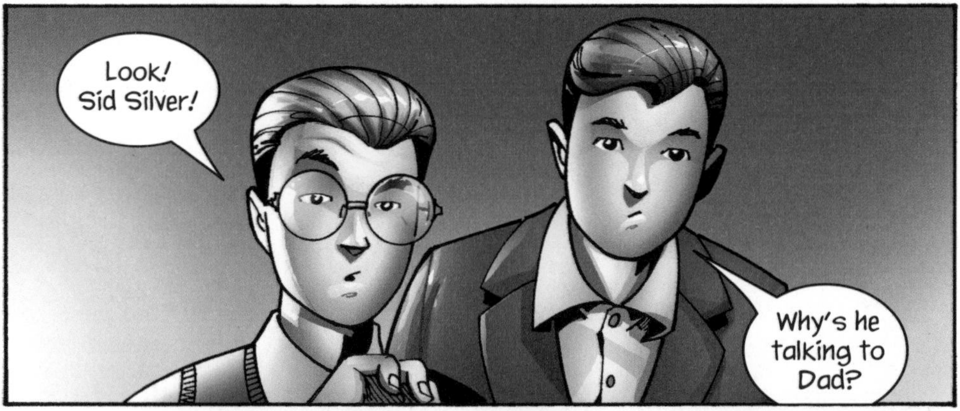
Look! Sid Silver!
Why's he talking to Dad?

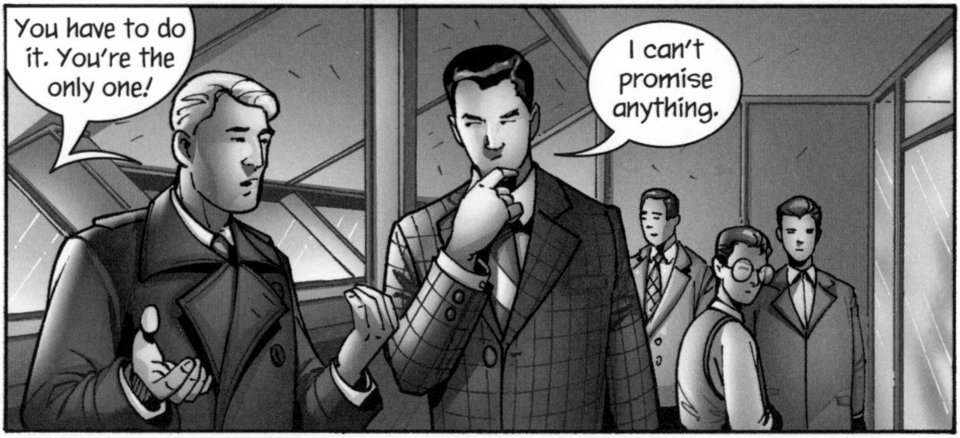
You have to do it. You're the only one!
I can't promise anything.

Dad stopped talking when he saw us. He looked worried for a second, then a grin spread across his face. "Just in time for liftoff!" Dad said.

Sid Silver scowled at us, turned, and walked quickly down the corridor. Peter and I looked at each other. Then Peter shrugged as if it were no big deal.

In an instant, I forgot all about the suspicious blond man. The *Hindenburg* was ready to rise into the sky. Below us, the ground crew untied the thick cables. A brass band played and spectators cheered. It was the first flight of 1937, and hundreds of people had come out to celebrate.

We lifted higher and higher, past the tops of trees and the roofs of buildings. I expected to feel a lurch in my stomach, like the kind you get when you ride an elevator. I felt nothing, as though we were perfectly still and the ground was moving away.

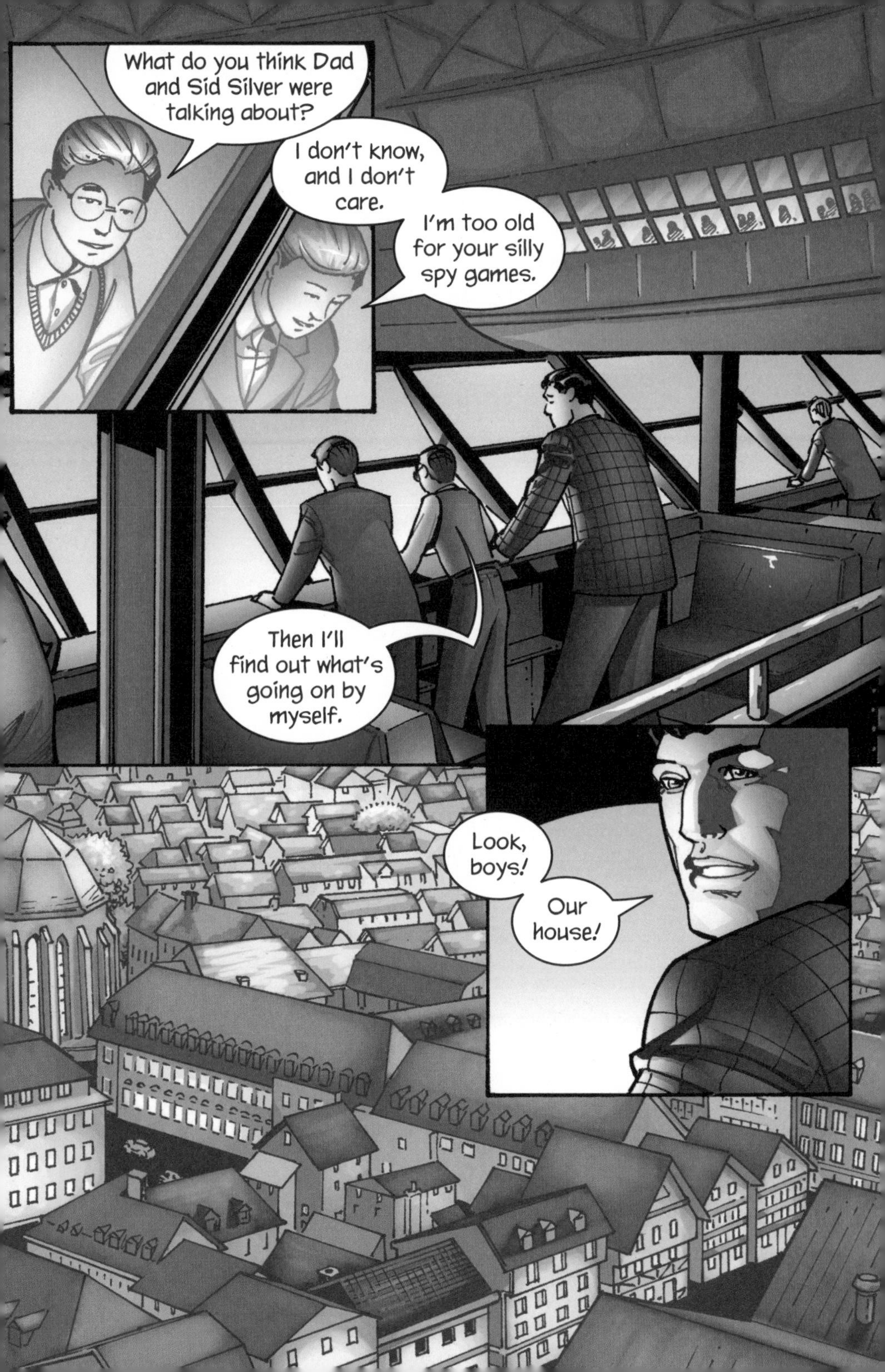
What do you think Dad and Sid Silver were talking about?
I don't know, and I don't care.
I'm too old for your silly spy games.
Then I'll find out what's going on by myself.
Look, boys!
Our house!

Just then, I saw a small figure on the street below. He was looking into the sky and waving.

It was Hans Bernstein, my old best friend, the boy I'd never gotten a chance to say good-bye to.

I waved back, but I don't think he saw me.

CHAPTER 5

THE MYSTERIOUS MEETING

"This is the kitchen where all the meals are cooked," said Dr. Rudiger.

I gave a bored sigh. We were on a tour of the *Hindenburg*, but so far the ship's doctor and our tour guide had only shown us places we could see for ourselves.

As if he could sense my boredom, Dr. Rudiger announced, "Now I'm going to take you somewhere that only *Hindenburg* officials are allowed."

He unlocked a door and ushered us inside. We stood on a long metal walkway. "Look up," Dr. Rudiger said.

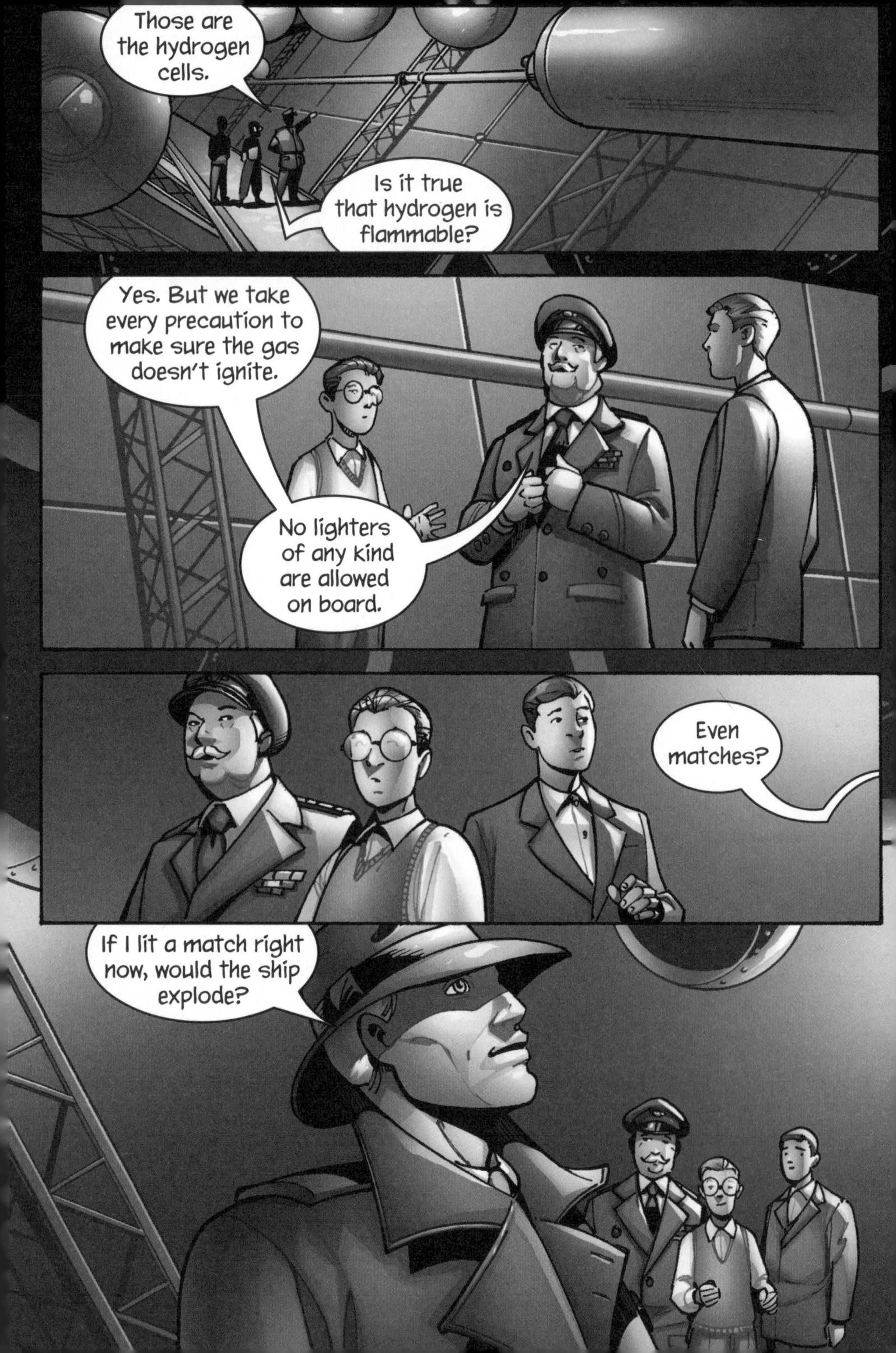
Those are the hydrogen cells.
Is it true that hydrogen is flammable?
Yes. But we take every precaution to make sure the gas doesn't ignite.
No lighters of any kind are allowed on board.
Even matches?
If I lit a match right now, would the ship explode?

Dr. Rudiger looked nervous. "You shouldn't have any matches, sir," he said. "And even if you did, the hydrogen is sealed tight inside these cells."

Peter seemed satisfied, but I was not. I stared up at the hydrogen cells. *What if one of the cells were punctured or leaked?* I wondered. *It wouldn't take much to set the* Hindenburg *on fire.*

"Tour's over," Dr. Rudiger said, giving a stern look at Sid Silver.

I nudged Peter. "See!" I said.

Peter only shook his head disgustedly.

As we slowly walked down the hall to our usual spot at the windows, I thought aloud. "If someone really wanted to blow up the ship, it wouldn't be very hard."

Peter sighed. "There you go again!" he said. "You're as suspicious as Hitler!"

A few minutes later, we were rounding the corner near the dining room. Suddenly, Peter stopped. He gripped my arm.

I could see two figures in the dining room, hunched over a table. It was Dad and Sid Silver.

Sid passed a piece of paper to Dad. Dad looked at it and passed it back. Sid stared at the paper, shaking his head. Then he slammed his fist against the table so hard I thought the *Hindenburg* would fall from the sky.

Sid glanced around him and quickly stuffed the paper into his pocket. "We have to get it right!" he said.

We shrank back into the shadows. "What was on the paper?" Peter whispered. "Did you see?"

"No," I said. "It's too far away."

"Do you think it is plans for a bomb?" he asked.

I couldn't help but smile. Finally Peter had realized something strange was going on.

I shrugged. "Whatever it was, they sure were studying it closely," I said.

Over the next two days, we often saw my father and Sid Silver together. But we came no closer to seeing what was on that mysterious piece of paper. We tried to sneak up on them, but they always spotted us before we got close.

On Wednesday, I was walking from our cabin to the lounge. On the way, I heard voices.

"T. H. E." my father said.

"T. H. E.," Sid repeated. "I will get it. I will get it soon."

I scurried back to the cabin and woke Peter.

"T. H. E.?" Peter said after I'd told him what I'd heard. "Sounds like the ingredients for a bomb."

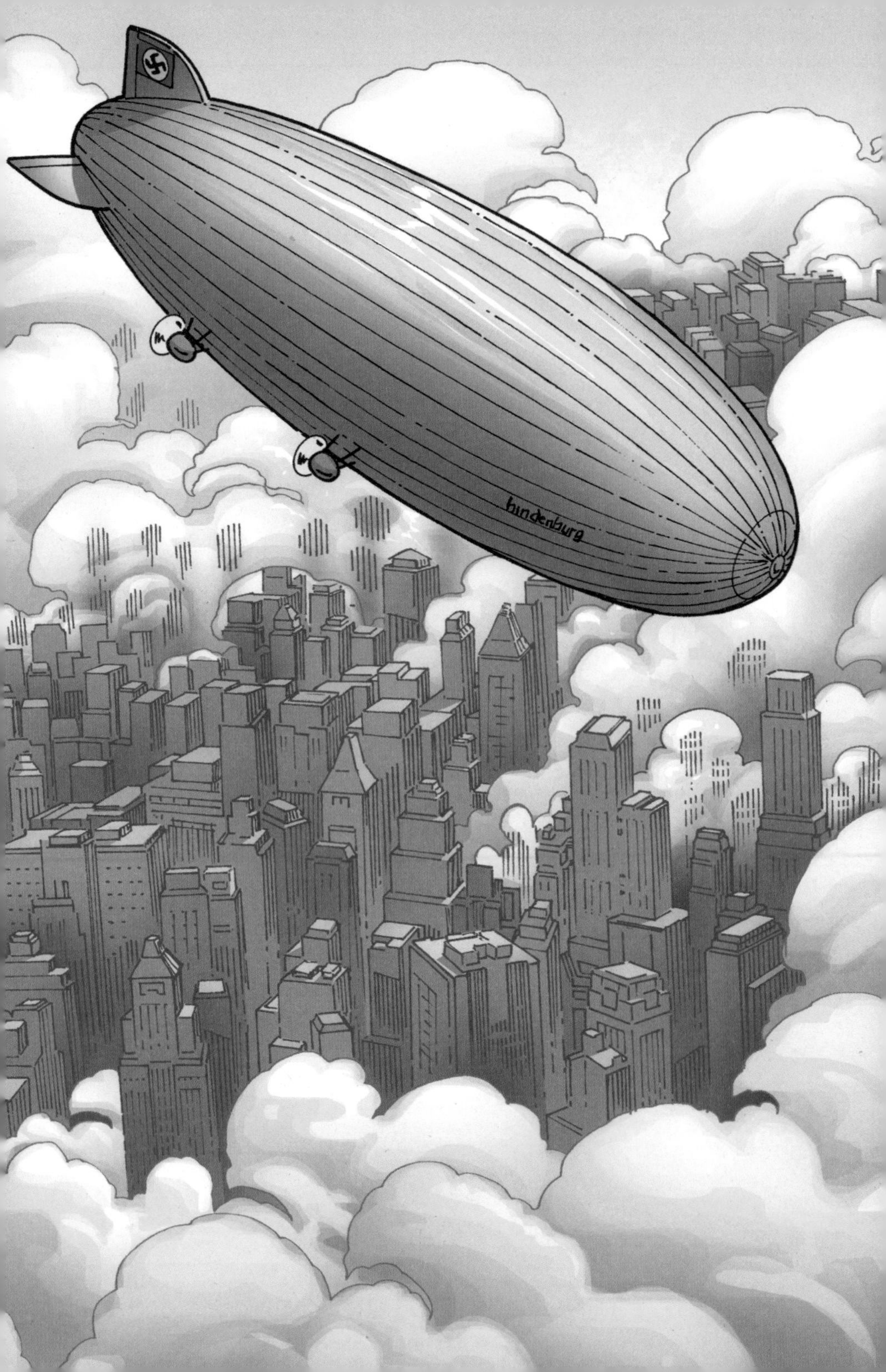
hindenburg

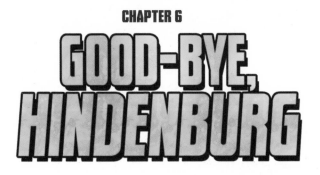

CHAPTER 6

GOOD-BYE, HINDENBURG

In the morning, we awoke to a drizzly gray sky. The clouds clustered around and blocked our view of the ocean below.

Then we broke through the clouds to the most spectacular sight we'd ever seen: New York City!

Tall buildings covered the ground below us like a maze. One building nearly touched us as we passed. It was the Empire State Building, the tallest building in the world.

"Home," Dad said.

We'd be landing soon, so Peter and I rushed to get our bags. I felt a twinge of sadness to be leaving the *Hindenburg*. But I knew that more exciting adventures lay below in America.

I looked at the Ghost of the *Titanic*, my model ship, before putting it into my bag. "You made it this time," I said.

I shouldn't have spoken so soon. Hours passed, and we still hadn't landed.

"There have been lightning storms in the area," Dad explained.

Sid Silver didn't leave the windows. He glanced at his watch over and over, sighing and looking worried.

Near seven o'clock, Captain Pruss announced that we'd be landing shortly. I looked out the window. Sure enough, I could see the airfield at Lakehurst, New Jersey.

"What makes the *Hindenburg* come down?" I asked Dad.

"Hydrogen is released out the back of the ship to make the *Hindenburg* heavier," he explained.

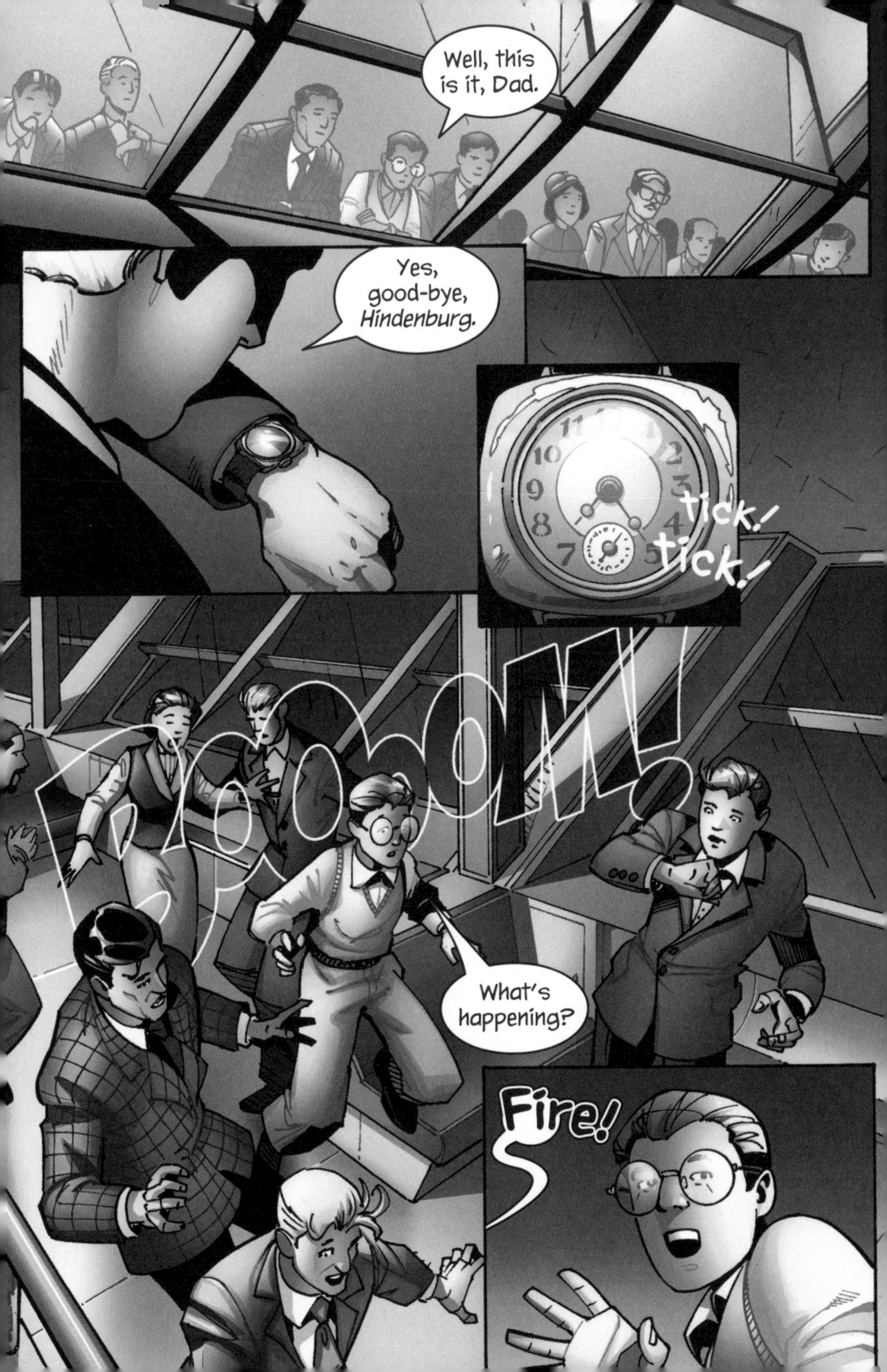
Well, this is it, Dad.
Yes, good-bye, Hindenburg.
tick! tick!
BOOOOM!
What's happening?
Fire!

A crowd of passengers surged against me, swallowing up Dad and Peter. "Dad!" I yelled. I could not hear his voice among the screams.

The *Hindenburg* tilted. Below, the ground crew was scattering, running away from the ship.

"Jump, kid, or I'll throw you out," growled Sid Silver from behind me.

I was pressed so closely against the windows that I couldn't move. The ground drew closer, but it was still too far to jump. The spectators along the fence screamed. The other passengers around me screamed. I realized that I was screaming, too.

It was too far to jump, my mind said. But my body burned with the fire that was sweeping down the hall. "Get out!" another person shouted.

I remembered what Father had said about disasters: "Don't fear the future. Embrace life."

I pulled myself up to the window and jumped.

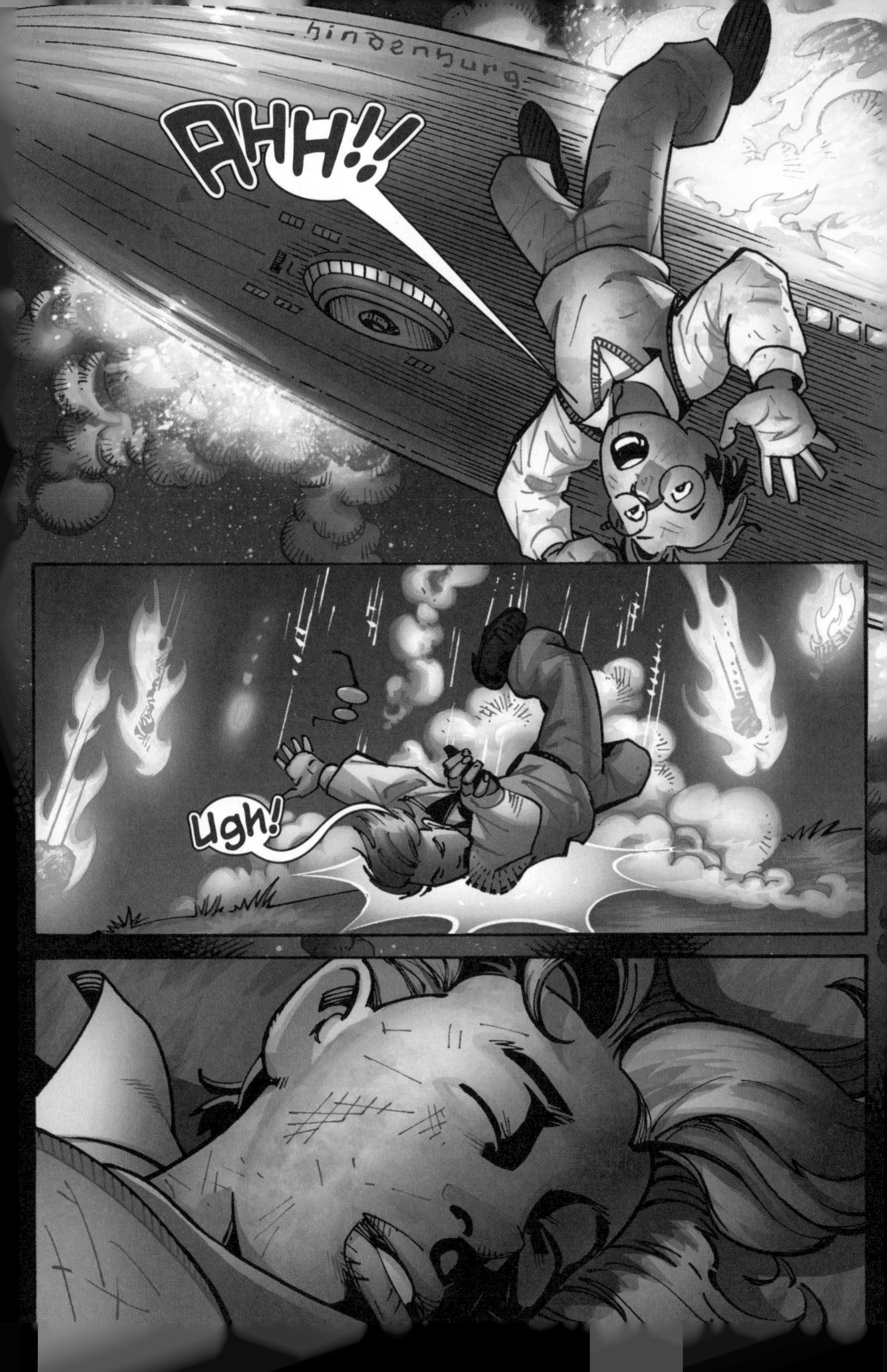
hindenburg
AHH!!
Ugh!

Shouts on the airfield quickly awakened me. Tears burned my eyes, hotter than the smoke of the *Hindenburg*. But I didn't even stop to check if I was hurt. I leaped to my feet.

"Dad!" I screamed. "Peter!" I saw neither of them.

What would happen if Dad and Peter were dead? I wondered. *I'd be left in America all alone. What would I do?*

The *Hindenburg* was a burning red blaze. The great luxury airship, the glistening silver wave of the future, was crumbling to ashes. A bolt of flame shot out its nose. Then I saw a flaming figure jump from one of the windows.

"Peter!" I raced toward him. He fell to the ground, flames leaping from his back. I charged at him, tackled him, and rolled with him until the flames were out.

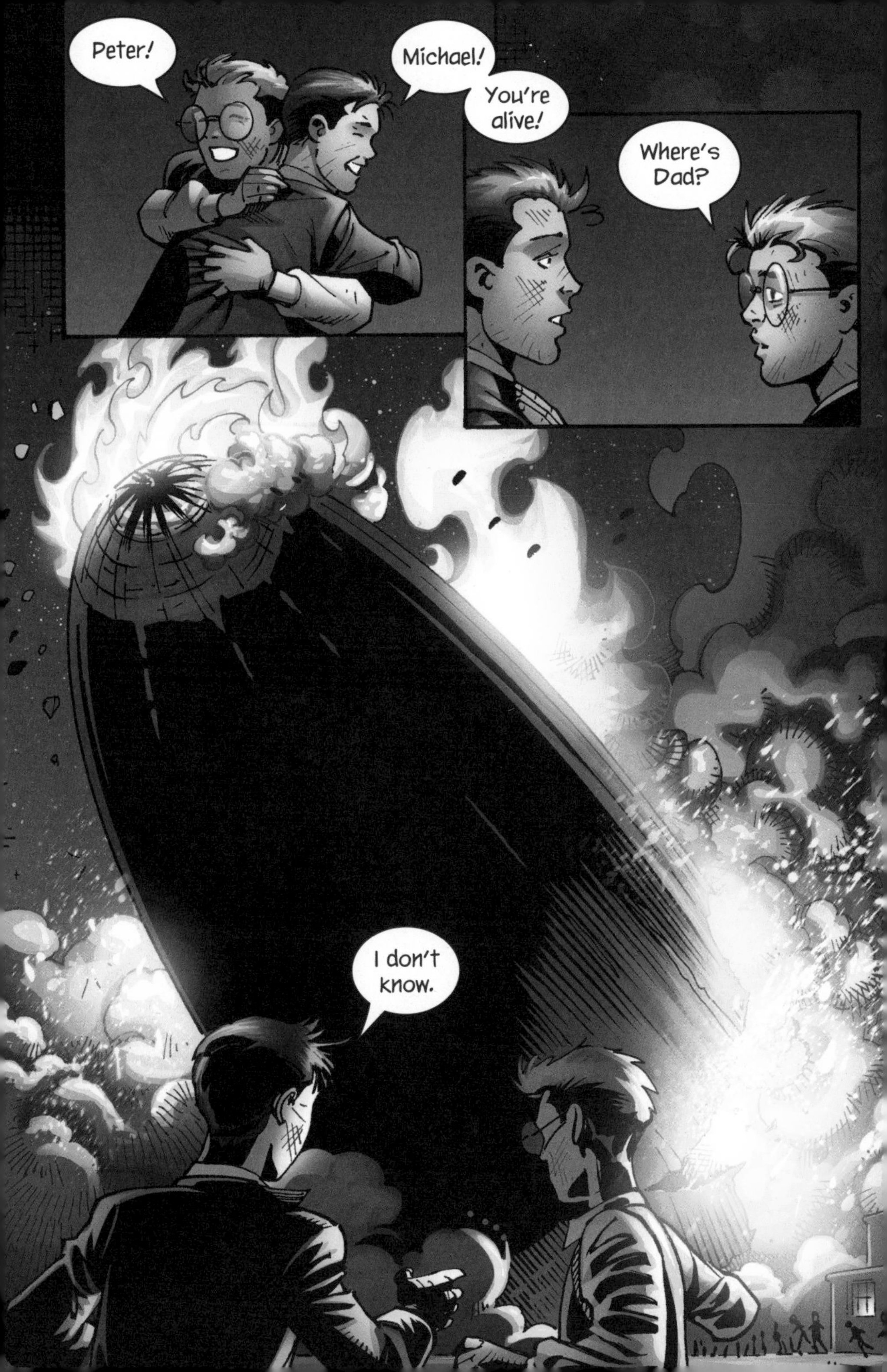
Peter!
Michael!
You're alive!
Where's Dad?
I don't know.

CHAPTER 7

SID THE SPY

I settled Peter on the floor of the hangar, where injured passengers were being treated. Then I went out to find Dad.

The smoke outside was so thick I couldn't see anything. Firemen rushed past me. "Dad? Dad?" I yelled.

Then I heard a voice through the shouts and cries of others on the ground. "Michael? Over here!"

I coughed my way toward the voice.

Dad was kneeling on the ground next to a burned, charred figure. He jumped up when he saw me and gave me a hug.

"Oh, thank goodness," he said. "But Peter?"

"Peter's fine," I said. I glanced at the figure on the ground. His blond hair was streaked with ash. His dark eyes were closed. It was Sid Silver.

"Is he dead?" I asked.

Just then, Sid gave a low cough. He moaned and rolled in agony. Something slipped from his pocket.

The mysterious paper! The paper looked charred and burned, but I snatched it before Dad could see it and shoved it into my pocket.

"What started the fire? Was it a bomb?" I demanded.

Sid moaned again. Dad shook his head. "I don't know," he said. "We might never know."

I felt the paper in my pocket. *I might already have the answer,* I thought.

Rescue workers came to carry Sid into the hangar. Dad and I followed slowly. I tried not to look at the *Hindenburg*, now a sad skeleton.

An eerie silence surrounded us. Gone were the screams and the hiss of the flames. I realized that the entire fire had lasted less than a minute.

Then I remembered what Sid had said just before the blaze exploded. "Good-bye, *Hindenburg*," he'd said, looking at his watch.

Had he planted a time bomb? Was this a message to Hitler, telling him that his country and his ships were not indestructible?

Peter met us at the door of the hangar. He wasn't crying anymore. "Only my clothes were burned," he said. "If you hadn't tackled me to put out the fire, I might have been history."

Dad went to find Sid. I pulled Peter away from the crowd.

I have the paper.
Let's see!
Dear Sid,
Every minute you are away from me passes by so slowly. I long for us to be together.
It's not a plan for a bomb! It's a love letter!
But I thought —
You thought Sid and I blew up the *Hindenburg*?

Dad shook his head sadly. "First Hitler suspects me," he said. "Now my sons do."

I tossed the letter at Dad. "I just can't figure out what you had to do with this," I said. "Who is the letter from?"

Dad's smile was real this time. "Sid met a Jewish woman in Germany," he said. "They fell in love. She wrote him this letter."

"That's all?" I asked.

"And I helped him read it," Dad replied. "You see, Sid can't read. He never learned how."

"You were teaching him to read?" I squeaked.

Dad laughed. "Yes," he said. "He wanted to learn to read so he could write back to her. He wants to bring her to America, away from Hitler."

I thought of Hans, my best friend. He was Jewish, too. What would happen to him?

I felt lucky as I looked around at the wounded. "I didn't want to jump," I told Dad. "But I thought about what you've always told us about surviving the *Titanic*."

"Don't fear the future. Embrace life," he said.

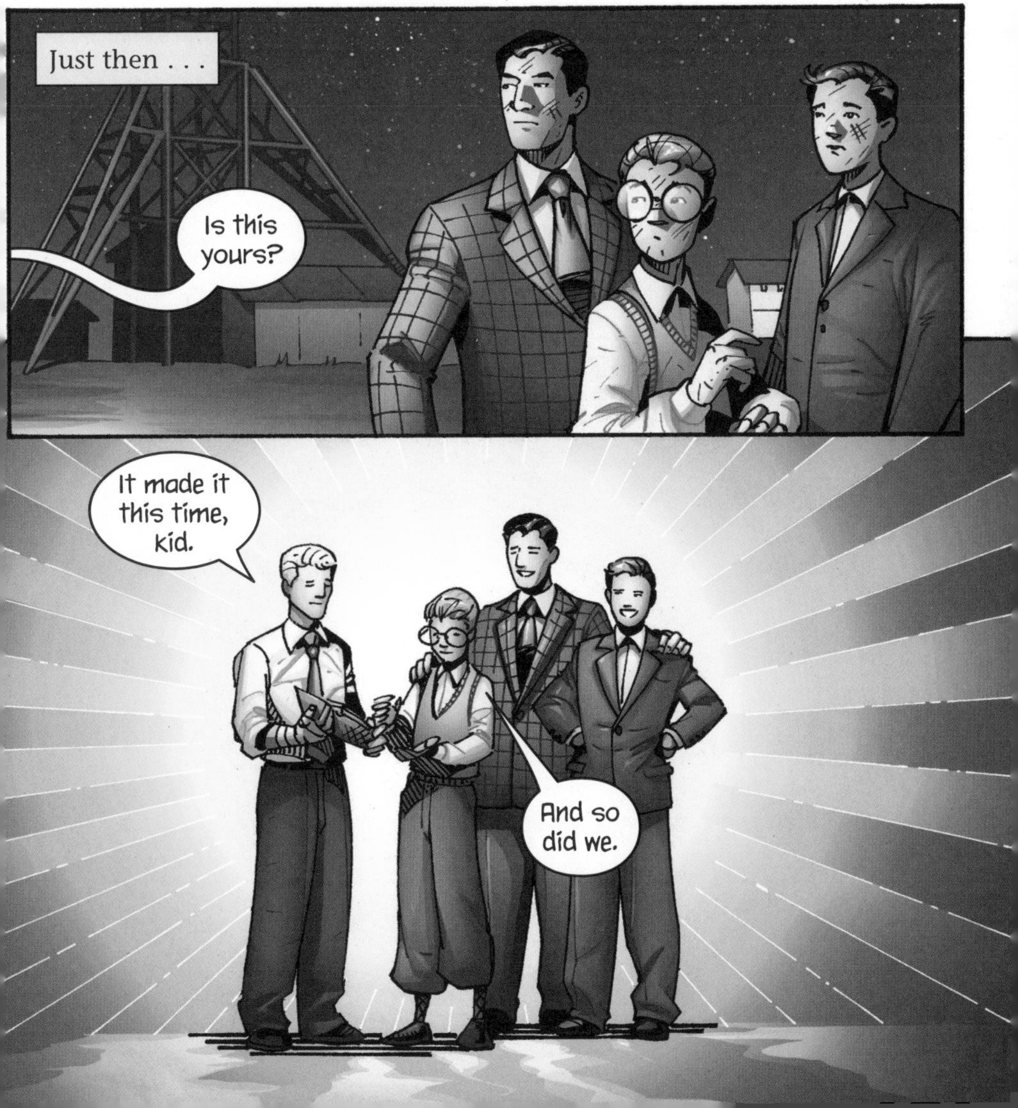
Just then . . .
Is this yours?
It made it this time, kid.
And so did we.

ABOUT THE AUTHOR

Jessica Gunderson grew up in the small town of Washburn, North Dakota. She has a bachelor's degree from the University of North Dakota and a master's degree in creative writing from Minnesota State University, Mankato. She likes rainy days and thunderstorms. She also likes exploring haunted houses and playing Mad Libs. She teaches English in Madison, Wisconsin, where she lives with her cat, Yossarian.

ABOUT THE ILLUSTRATOR

Claude St. Aubin was born in Ontario, Canada. He went to college in Montreal, Quebec, where he graduated with a degree in graphic design. After working for a Canadian comic book publisher for a short time, St. Aubin pursued a career as a graphic designer. Soon, however, he returned to his true passion as a comic book artist. St. Aubin is happily married with two children.

GLOSSARY

abrupt (uh-BRUPT)—sudden and unexpected

awe (AW)—an overwhelming feeling of amazement

disgustedly (dis-GHUST-id-lee)—with distaste or loathing

embraced (em-BRAYSSD)—held tightly

indestructible (in-di-STRUHK-tuh-buhl)—unable to be destroyed

port (PORT)—the left-hand side of a ship or an aircraft

precaution (pri-KAW-shuhn)—something you do to guard against something dangerous

scowled (SKOULD)—made an angry frown

starboard (STAR-burd)—the right-hand side of a ship or an aircraft

traitor (TRAY-tur)—someone who betrays something

ushered (UHSH-urd)—led or guided someone

wobbled (WOB-uhld)—moved unsteadily

MORE ABOUT THE HINDENBURG

The *Hindenburg* was built in Germany in 1936. The airship was almost three football fields long and could carry 70 passengers and 61 crew members. It traveled nearly 90 miles per hour!

The *Hindenburg* was filled with hydrogen. Hydrogen is a gas that is lighter than air, which allowed the zeppelin to float while engines propelled it forward. The danger of the ship's design was that hydrogen is flammable, so any sparks or flames could ignite the ship.

On May 3, 1937, the *Hindenburg* took off from Germany and headed for New Jersey. The trip was delayed due to bad weather, which forced the zeppelin to take a scenic detour of New York. Eventually, the weather settled down, and the *Hindenburg* finally prepared to land.

The crowd of people watching the landing noticed sparks toward the rear of the ship. Seconds later, the hydrogen gas ignited. It took about 34 seconds for the *Hindenburg* to become consumed in flames. Surprisingly, most of the ship's crew and passengers survived. Of the 97 people onboard when the zeppelin caught fire, 35 people died.

No one knows for certain what caused the *Hindenburg* to catch fire. Some suspect electricity caused by static, lightning, or sparks from the engines ignited the hydrogen gas. The flames then spread to the rest of the ship.

The disaster could have been avoided if the designers of the *Hindenburg* had used the non-flammable gas helium in place of hydrogen. At the time, however, the United States was the main supplier of helium. The U.S. government refused to give the gas to Germany because they opposed the Nazi party.

DISCUSSION QUESTIONS

1. What do you think about Mrs. Roth's rule that the boys could not be friends with Jewish people? Why did she believe this was an important rule?

2. Michael says the swastikas displayed around town and on the *Hindenburg* frighten him. Why? What did they symbolize?

3. What characteristics did Sid Silver have that made Michael suspicious of him?

WRITING PROMPTS

1. The book doesn't explain how Mr. Roth, an American, came to live in Germany. Write a story that tells this tale.

2. Mrs. Roth planned to take a ship to join her family in the United States. Write a description of the ship.

3. Imagine Michael had gotten a chance to say good-bye to his old friend Hans Bernstein before he left. Write this scene.

INTERNET SITES

Do you want to know more about subjects related to this book? Or are you interested in learning about other topics? Then check out FactHound, a fun, easy way to find Internet sites.

Our investigative staff has already sniffed out great sites for you!

Here's how to use FactHound:

1. Visit *www.facthound.com*

2. Select your grade level.

3. To learn more about subjects related to this book, type in the book's ISBN number: 9781434211637.

4. Click the Fetch It button.

FactHound will fetch the best Internet sites for you.